The Adventures of Sarah Elizabeth and Jason T. Bear

Elizabeth Wright

HAPPY READING! ♡
BEAR HUGS,
ELIZABETH WRIGHT

"The Adventures of Sarah Elizabeth and Jason T. Bear," by Elizabeth Wright. ISBN 978-1-62137-646-0 (softcover), 978-1-62137-647-7 (ebook).

Library of Congress Control Number on file with publisher.

Manufactured in the United States of America.

For my wonderful husband, children, and grandchildren
who share my love of writing, reading, dolls, and teddy bears.

Adventures at the Beach

CHAPTER 1
A Soggy Surprise

Sarah Elizabeth brushed a dark curl from her eyes as she looked out at the ocean. A strange object was bobbing up and down in the water. It seemed to be coming closer to the beach.

She knew it wasn't seaweed, and it didn't look like driftwood. It certainly wasn't big enough to be an otter or a seal.

What could it be?

Suddenly, a huge wave picked it up, and with a rush and whirl of white foam, flung it at Sarah Elizabeth's feet. The doll could hardly believe her eyes.

"It's a BEAR!" she shouted. "It's the muddiest, wettest, soggiest teddy bear I've ever seen."

She reached for her towel and began to dry it, starting with its water-soaked paws. As she dried the bear, its fur began to glisten in the sunshine. Then she noticed that it had a gold chain with a medal around its neck. On the medal, she saw the words: "JASON T. BEAR, TIME-TRAVELER."

As she began to dry his ears, the bear gave an enormous sigh and opened his eyes. "Who are you? Where am I?" he asked.

"I'm Sarah Elizabeth, and this is a beach in California. Did you fall out of a boat?"

The bear shook his head, splashing water on her white pinafore apron. "Oops! Sorry about that. Pleased to meet you, Sarah Elizabeth. I am Jason T. Bear, Time-Traveler. This is most extraordinary – absolutely never happened before! Must be one of King Neptune's tricks. Last I recall, we were playing a game of seashells in the crystal palace, with mermaids and seahorses everywhere. Now here I am on a beach in California, having my ears dried by a lovely doll. What a surprise! What a smashing surprise! Sarah Elizabeth, how may I return your kindness?"

"Oh, Mr. Bear, you needn't do that. You would have helped me if you had found me half-drowned and soaking wet. Do you really know the King of the Oceans?"

"Yes, Sarah Elizabeth, King Neptune and I have been friends for a very long time, centuries in fact. He's a grand old fellow, but he does love his jokes." The bear stood up, giving himself a shake as he did so. A little flurry of ocean drops scattered through the air. "Time to be off, my dear, but we will meet again soon, and when we do, your life will change in a most exciting way. Jason T. Bear always returns a favor."

The bear walked off down the beach at a rapid pace, disappearing so quickly that Sarah Elizabeth wondered if she'd been dreaming. She picked up her towel and started for home.

As she walked, she tried to remember everything that had happened from the moment she'd seen Jason T. Bear in the water. Questions flew through her mind.

Why did her towel look so clean? The bear had been a muddy mess when she'd dried him with it. Could Jason T. Bear really know King Neptune? What did "Time-Traveler" mean? Would she ever see the bear again?

(If Sarah Elizabeth had looked above, in the tall pine tree near her gate, she would have seen something furry watching her. Instead, she hurried through the gate and on up the stairs.)

Tuptim, a plump, Siamese cat was waiting for her by the door. The cat looked at her with her big blue eyes and meowed softly.

CHAPTER 2
The Home on the Hill

Sarah Elizabeth's home was on a hill overlooking the small beach town. It had a wonderful view of both mountains and ocean. The doll loved walking about the garden, making bouquets of wild roses and forget-me-nots. It was always a thrill when hummingbirds put on a show for her. She'd stand very still while they darted about the flowers, their ruby and emerald colors flashing in the sunlight.

The house was large but cozy inside. Bright blue curtains framed the windows, and a large blue and white rug covered part of the wooden floor. Walls were hung with pictures from long ago. Shelves and tables were filled with books, seashells and pine cones. There was an antique phonograph in one corner of the room and an old upright piano in another. A beautiful brick fireplace gave warmth to the house in cold weather.

It was around this fireplace that the professors, Drew and Kate, worked each evening, he correcting history papers and she writing her latest book.

Sarah Elizabeth had her own little chair nearby. She loved sitting with the professors, reading a favorite book, writing in her diary or listening to them talking. Sometimes they would tell stories about the town during the old days, when everyone lived in tents or small cottages. Tonight, they were reading a letter from their daughter, Kristi, who was away at the university.

The Adventures of Sarah Elizabeth and Jason T. Bear

Sarah Elizabeth and Kristi had been together since Kristi's sixth birthday, when the doll had arrived in a big box with a gold ribbon. After all of those years together, she thought she'd be going with Kristi to the university. It had been a shock to learn she had to stay home to keep the professors and Tuptim from being lonely.

It had been Sarah Elizabeth's dream to study languages so she could travel and speak with dolls in other countries. Sometimes, she even wished she could travel back in time to meet the great women and men of long ago.

Sarah Elizabeth began to write in her diary:

Dear Diary,

I met the most amazing bear today. I won't tell the professors yet. I want to tell Kristi first. I miss her so much. I wonder if I'll ever get to the university?

I don't think the professors will have time to be lonely. If only I could find a friend for Tuptim.

Love,
Sarah Elizabeth

Later as she was getting ready for bed, she found a beautiful seashell in her pocket. She started to put it on the bureau and then saw that it had the initials, "J.T.B." on it.

Jason T. Bear, thought Sarah Elizabeth. Now she knew she hadn't been dreaming.

(If she'd looked toward her window, she would have seen a furry face looking in at her. Yes, it was Jason T. Bear, himself. He smiled a sweet smile and then vanished.)

CHAPTER 3
The Book Shop

In the morning, Sarah Elizabeth woke up early. It was a beautiful day. The sun was shining; the ocean was a brilliant blue. She dressed quickly so that she could take a walk before the book shop opened.

The doll loved to walk about the little town. There were so many quaint homes to see. Her favorite was the one that looked like Sleeping Beauty's castle. It was pale pink with a tower and was set back from the road with a high fence. She could peek between the fence slats to see it.

As she took her walk, she greeted the cats and dogs along her way. They responded with whisker-twitchings and tail-wags.

She called to a peacock sitting on a roof, and he waved his blue-green feathers at her.

By the time she reached the book shop, it was already open.

"Sarah Elizabeth, how are you this morning?" asked Emily, the shopkeeper.

"I'm fine, Emily, and you?"

"Perfect, on such a pretty day. What can I do for you?"

"I'm looking for a book about bears, Emily."

"Grizzlies, polar bears or koalas, Sarah Elizabeth?"

"None of those, Emily. I need one about teddy bears."

"Teddy bears? Let's look in the back of the store, dear. I think I have several books about them there."

(If Sarah Elizabeth had glanced up at the top bookshelf, she would have seen two bright eyes peering at her from behind a large book about redwood trees. She didn't look up though and missed seeing Jason T. Bear.)

Emily and Sarah Elizabeth looked carefully at the books which featured teddy bears. There were several about Little Bear, more about Winnie the Pooh, some about B. B. Bear and, of course, a few about Paddington. Emily said that she knew of another book all about teddy bears. If she wished, Emily would order a copy for her. Sarah Elizabeth said she'd like that very much and would be back soon.

The stores along the main street were all open now. Their owners waved to her as she went past. She smiled and greeted each one in turn. The flower lady gave her a pretty yellow tulip. The doll thanked her and carried it carefully as she walked along. She felt so happy that she began singing a little song to herself as she walked up the big hill.

When she finally reached her home again, she discovered a note from the professors:

Dear Sarah Elizabeth,

We've gone to the city to visit Cousin Theresa. Please feed Tuptim if we're late returning.

Love,
Drew & Kate

Sarah Elizabeth found a vase in the kitchen. She filled it with water and put her yellow tulip in it. Then she placed it on a table in the dining room. It looked very beautiful, and she hoped Kate would see it while it was still fresh.

CHAPTER 4
Travel Plans

Sarah Elizabeth had been reading for quite awhile. She was beginning to feel a bit drowsy. Kate and Drew were still gone. She heard a soft knock at the door, and looking up, saw Jason T. Bear through the window. Sarah Elizabeth hurried to the door and opened it.

"Come in, come in, Mr. Bear. I'm so happy to see you. Would you like a cup of tea? I was just about to have some tea and biscuits with honey. Please sit down."

"Ah, Sarah Elizabeth, tea and biscuits with honey will be most welcome. Sounds scrumptious! I've come to discuss a very interesting travel plan with you, and such a snack will help me think more clearly."

Jason settled himself in a chair as Sarah Elizabeth went to the kitchen, returning shortly with a tea tray. She poured the tea and passed the biscuits to Jason. Then she pulled up a chair and sat down facing him.

Jason T. Bear thumped a paw on the arm of his chair. "First things first, Sarah Elizabeth, I've decided that since we are going to know each other very well, we must shorten the forms of our names. You will call me Jason, and I will call you Sarabeth. This will be a big help in case of emergency. A bit informal perhaps, but very practical, indeed."

"All right, Mr. B…, I mean, Jason. It's a good idea."

"Sarabeth, it has come to my attention that you are a doll with a secret wish. My word, these biscuits are fine, and what delicious honey! Ah yes, you've always wanted to travel and even more, to travel back in time. Isn't that true?"

Sarah Elizabeth was stunned. "How did you find out, Jason? I've never told anyone."

"That will be my secret, Sarabeth. Would you like to hear my plan?"

"Oh yes, Jason. I can hardly wait."

Jason took a sip of his tea and finished another biscuit. Sarah Elizabeth sat on the edge of her chair.

"Now then, I'm quite used to time-travel, but for your first trip, I think we should only go back as far as the early 1900's." Jason rubbed his paws together and looked thoughtful. "Urrr, yes. That's it. We'll visit this very town. Would you like that, Sarabeth? How soon can you be ready?"

"Oh Jason, that sounds like so much fun. I'd love to go right now, but I'm supposed to feed Tuptim dinner, and I'm worried about her. Kristi left me here to keep Tuptim and the professors from feeling lonely. The professors will be fine since they have each other's company, but Tuptim needs a friend."

"No problem, my dear. Pull my left ear gently. Don't look worried. Just do as I say."

Sarah Elizabeth gave the bear's ear a little tug and instantly heard a "meow" at her feet. Looking down, she saw a silky black cat staring up at her with big golden eyes. Seconds later, Tuptim walked into the room. The two cats stared at each other, blue eyes inspecting gold eyes. The black cat gave a little bow.

They sniffed noses and circled each other gracefully. Then Tuptim bowed, and both cats walked to the door. Sarah Elizabeth got up and opened the door for them. Tuptim and her new friend walked down the stairway into the garden.

"Jason, you solved my problem! I'll leave some food on the porch for the cats. Then I'll write a note to the professors so they won't worry about me."

"Excellent, Sarabeth. A fine idea!"

Sarah Elizabeth put out the food, then got a pen and paper from the desk and wrote the following:

Darling Professors,

I have a chance to travel, but I must leave immediately. Tuptim has a new friend and won't miss me. I left food on the porch for both cats. Let's call the new one, "Blackberry."

Love and hugs,
Sarah Elizabeth

P.S. Tell Kristi I'll send her a postcard.

"Jason, will I need a coat or umbrella?"

"Neither, Sarabeth, you'll be fine as you are. Now hold my left paw while I say the magic words." Jason began to rub his gold medal with his right paw while he chanted in a low growly voice:

"Wings of gold and crystal bells,
Starlight in the night,
Take us swiftly through the years,
As we fade from sight."

CHAPTER 5
The Lost Ring

Sarah Elizabeth stood on the sand looking up and down the beach. Everything looked very different.

"Hmmm," she said to herself. "I wonder where Jason is? Last I remember, we were in my home, and he said some magic words. Oh my! Could it be?" Sarah Elizabeth rubbed her eyes. "There aren't any houses on the beach." She looked toward the hills and rubbed her eyes again.

Her home was gone, and there were only a few small cottages and tents to be seen on the lower part of the hills. Sarah Elizabeth pinched herself and wished very hard that Jason would hurry up and join her.

She saw a figure coming toward her and thought it must be Jason. As it came closer, she saw that it was a doll wearing an old-fashioned swimsuit. She seemed to be looking for something. Sarah Elizabeth could hear her crying and talking to herself.

"Oh dear! How could I have been so stupid? I'll never find it. It's lost forever. What should I do? I can't go home without it. If I don't find it soon, the tide will come in and sweep it out to sea." The doll began to sob.

Sarah Elizabeth forgot her own worries for the moment and said, "Excuse me, would you like me to help you find whatever you've lost?"

The doll jumped back in surprise. She'd been crying so hard she hadn't realized that she was nearly standing on Sarah Elizabeth. "Oh my! I'm ever so sorry. I almost stepped on you. What did you say?"

"I asked if you would let me help you hunt for whatever you've lost," said Sarah Elizabeth.

The doll wiped away a tear and gave a brave little smile. "That would be very kind of you. It's been such a bad week. First the horses backed our buggy off the road, and we were nearly killed. Then David cut his foot. And Amy's ring is lost. It's the one Aunt Lavinia gave her. I tried it on this morning and forgot I was wearing it. I think I must have lost it when I tried to keep Rosie from catching a sandpiper."

The doll's words had come out in a rush, and Sarah Elizabeth was very confused.

"Rosie, Amy, David? You lost a flower and cut your foot?"

"No, no, forgive me. I said it all too fast and muddled you up. Rosie is our Irish Setter. David cut his foot on a piece of glass at the beach, and I lost Amy's ring. I'm Jessica by the way."

Sarah Elizabeth smiled. "I'm beginning to understand, Jessica. My name is Sarah Elizabeth. I'd be happy to help you look for the ring. What does it look like?"

A tear slid down Jessica's nose. "It's gold with a real diamond." She began adjusting her sun hat, which had slipped down over one eye.

"Don't cry anymore, Jessica. I'm sure we'll find the ring, but if we don't, Jason will help us."

"Jason? Who's Jason?" asked Jessica.

"You will meet him soon. He's a good friend of mine." Sarah Elizabeth gave Jessica a hug. "Let's retrace your walk on the beach, Jessica. If we look carefully, we should find your ring."

The dolls had been searching for nearly an hour, trying not to miss any part of the sand. They had looked under seashells, driftwood and seaweed. It was beginning to seem hopeless.

While they'd been hunting for the ring, a thick gray fog had been rolling across the water. The air had grown colder; the sky was getting dark. Waves were reaching higher and higher on the sand. Jessica suddenly realized what had happened.

"Come quickly, Sarah Elizabeth. We must leave the beach at once or we won't be able to find the path. If the tide comes any higher, it will sweep us out to the ocean." Jessica was obviously frightened. "Take my hand, and we'll run together," she cried.

They began to run, but it was nearly impossible in the deep sand. The fog was closing fast about them. It was so thick that they could only see a few steps ahead.

"How far do we have to go, Jessica?"

"We should have come to the old log that marks the path by now. If we've gone past it, I don't know what we'll do. Oh no! Look at the waves!"

Just at that moment, there was a whirring sound in the fog, and Jason T. Bear appeared before them. "Beastly weather, my dears! May I be of some assistance?"

"Look, Jessica. It's Jason T. Bear! Jason, this is my new friend, Jessica. Thank goodness you're here. I've been trying to help her find Amy's ring, but the tide is coming in, and the fog is so thick we can't find the path."

"No problem, no problem at all." Jason T. Bear raised his paw and twitched his nose. As he did so, the fog lifted to reveal a huge log, and next to it, a path. Sarah Elizabeth was getting used to Jason's powers, but Jessica widened her eyes in amazement.

"Follow me, no time to lose. Your family is worried about you, Jessica." Jason T. Bear led the girls up the path, past a group of tents, and on up the road leading to Jessica's little cottage.

Just as they reached the porch, Jason T. Bear said, "I must be off now. Ta ta, pip pip and all that, till we meet again." The dolls stared at each other. Jason had departed as swiftly as he'd arrived.

CHAPTER 6
A Familiar Family

The door was slightly ajar. Jessica gave it a push, and as they stepped inside, a young girl cried out, "Jessica! Where have you been? Mama, my doll is home, and she's brought someone with her. Jessica, we were so worried about you. Papa and the boys are out looking for you. What happened? You look exhausted." The girl picked her up in her arms.

Jessica's chin quivered. Her eyes began to fill. "Oh Amy, you'll never speak to me again. I couldn't find it anywhere. This is Sarah Elizabeth. She was kind enough to help me. We looked and looked all over the beach, but the fog came in, and we couldn't find the path. If her friend hadn't rescued us, we'd still be lost."

"It's lovely to meet you, Sarah Elizabeth. Now let's all go into the kitchen where it is warmer. I want Mama to hear this."

As they passed the living room, Sarah Elizabeth noticed that there were books everywhere. In one corner was a bright and shiny "morning glory" phonograph that reminded her of the old one at home.

In the kitchen, a pretty woman was standing near the sink slicing peaches. The room was warm, and Sarah Elizabeth could smell something delicious baking in the oven.

"Mama, here is Jessica and her new friend, Sarah Elizabeth. Sarah Elizabeth, this is my mother, Mrs. Scott."

"It's nice to meet you, Mrs. Scott." Sarah Elizabeth thought that this lovely woman seemed very familiar.

"Jessica, I'm so relieved that you are home. Do sit down, Sarah Elizabeth. I'm delighted to meet you. Amy, please get some sweaters and blankets. These poor little darlings are shivering. I do hope that John and the boys will be home soon. It's much too dark and foggy for anyone to be out now."

Amy quickly returned with soft woolen blankets and two cozy sweaters for the dolls. She helped settle them at the kitchen table and sat down with them.

"Now then, Jessica, tell me everything."

Jessica was trying hard not to cry again and looked at Sarah Elizabeth for extra courage. "Dear Amy, this morning after breakfast, I tried on your favorite ring, the one Aunt Lavinia gave you, but then I forgot I was wearing it." Jessica gave a big gulp and bravely went on. "Rosie and I went for a walk on the beach. She kept running up and down trying to catch sandpipers so I chased her, and she ran home. Then as I was walking home, I remembered your ring, and it was gone. It must have fallen in the sand. I'm so ashamed." Jessica gave a great sigh and put her head in her hands. "I went back to the beach and looked for it all day. That was when I met Sarah Elizabeth, and she's been helping me ever since. Could you tell the rest, Sarah Elizabeth?"

"Of course I will. Well, Jessica and I searched for a long time, up and down the beach, looking everywhere under seashells, stones and driftwood. Then the tide began to rise, a great wall of fog came rolling in, and we were lost ourselves." Sarah Elizabeth shivered remembering. "It was very cold and scary. Luckily, my good friend Jason arrived and found the path for us."

Amy hugged each doll. "Thank you for helping Jessica, Sarah Elizabeth. What a dreadful experience! Jessica, I know you didn't mean to lose the ring. Tomorrow, we'll put up a sign, asking everyone in town to help us find it."

Just as Amy said this, the door was flung open, and a man, two boys and a large dog rushed into the house. The boys were carrying wood, which they put in a box near the fireplace. The older boy began to build a fire. The man and younger boy came into the kitchen with the dog following.

"No luck this evening, we've looked everywhere. We'll have to wait until morning to start hunting again."

"Papa, look!" cried Amy. "Jessica is back, and this is her new friend, Sarah Elizabeth. They've had a terrible time, and I know that Jessica is very sorry you spent so much time looking for her."

Tears were sliding down Jessica's nose again. Rosie, the Irish setter, gave Jessica several large, slurpy licks.

"Don't cry, Jessica," said Mr. Scott. "I'm glad you are home safe and sound. How do you do, Sarah Elizabeth? This is our son, David."

"How do you do, Mr. Scott and David? It's nice to meet you both." Rosie was sniffing Sarah Elizabeth's hand and wagging her tail. "It's good to meet you, too, Rosie."

"Papa," said Mrs. Scott, "I've been keeping the food warm. Your favorites: chicken and dumplings, corn and apple pie. It will be ready as soon as you and the boys clean up."

During the meal, Amy told Sarah Elizabeth all about the town's costume party which would take place on the weekend. Once she decided who she wanted to be, the family would help her with her costume.

Later on, Amy played the piano while the family joined in singing with her. Seeing the family together, made Sarah Elizabeth think of some photos she'd seen in an old album at home. It suddenly dawned on her that these dear people were the same ones in those pictures and were related to her very own family.

She remembered that Professor Drew loved to tell about his father and grandparents when they first came to the beach town for their summers. Sarah Elizabeth couldn't wait to tell Jason.

As it was getting late, Mrs. Scott said, "Time for bed, children. Papa has to catch the stagecoach early in the morning to go to the city. We'll all be busy tomorrow sewing our outfits for the costume party. Amy will help you little ladies get ready for bed. Good night, dear ones."

(Do you think that anyone saw a furry gray shape behind the rocking chair?)

CHAPTER 7
The Old Oak Tree

By the time Sarah Elizabeth woke up the next morning, Mr. Scott had already left on the stagecoach and Mrs. Scott was making the breakfast. The boys were picking blackberries in the garden with Rosie's help. She loved to eat the berries from the vine, but she was careful not to let the thorns prick her nose.

Jessica was still asleep, but Sarah Elizabeth decided not to waken her since she could use the extra sleep to recover from yesterday. Sarah Elizabeth found Amy working on her poster. She had carefully printed the following:

LOST!
Tuesday – August 30, 1910
Gold and Diamond Ring
(My favorite, given to me by Aunt Lavinia.)
Please help me find it!
Amy Scott

"What do you think, Sarah Elizabeth?" asked Amy.

"It's perfect, Amy. Would you like me to go with you when you put it up?"

"Oh yes, Sarah Elizabeth. Let's ask Mama if we have time before breakfast."

Breakfast was a half hour away, so Amy and Sarah Elizabeth took the poster, a hammer and two nails and headed for the old oak tree which served as the town bulletin board.

Walking through the town gave Sarah Elizabeth such an odd feeling. There was nothing familiar at all. No bookstore, no fire station, no market, no ice cream stand. When they reached the tree, they discovered several notices on it already:

Wanted – a purple shawl
Needed – a parasol
Does anyone have a lace fan?
FREE kittens - Contact Miss Smith
FOR SALE – Wood, cheap price. Ask Mr. Brown

There was a large basket next to the tree with a purple shawl in it.

"Look Sarah Elizabeth, someone has already answered one of the requests. I wonder if Mama has a lace fan or a parasol? We'll have to look when we go home. I wish we could have a kitten, but Papa would say no because of Rosie." Amy began nailing her poster to the tree.

Sarah Elizabeth loved the "tree bulletin board" and the costume exchange. The families that lived in the town seemed to trust and look out for each other. Amy took it for granted that someone would find and return her ring to her. Sarah Elizabeth hoped she'd have a chance to talk about this with Jason T. Bear.

(Did you already guess? Yes, high, high up in the branches of the old oak tree Jason T. Bear was deep in thought.)

CHAPTER 8
An Enormous Emergency

When Sarah Elizabeth and Amy returned to the house, Rosie greeted them at the door. They were just in time for a breakfast of eggs, muffins, milk and fresh blackberries. Sarah Elizabeth remembered her new little cat, Blackberry, and hoped that all was well at home.

After breakfast, it was clean-up time. The boys and Rosie were sent to the beach to search for the ring. Sarah Elizabeth was surprised to find that Mrs. Scott had to heat water on the stove to wash the dishes. The house had no hot water, and she noticed that there wasn't a dishwasher or a refrigerator. She saw that foods, such as milk and butter, were kept on the kitchen porch in a large wooden box filled with a huge chunk of ice. Sarah Elizabeth had already noticed that there wasn't a radio, telephone or television in the house.

When the housework was done, Mrs. Scott, Amy and the dolls began to talk about the costume party. Amy told her mother about the requests on the oak tree. Mrs. Scott thought she could lend her parasol. Jessica wanted to be a princess and Sarah Elizabeth said she'd like to be Cleopatra. Amy wanted to be Juliet from "Romeo and Juliet."

"I know that Papa and the boys will need some help with their costumes," said Mrs. Scott. "Papa wants to be Robin Hood. George hopes to be Abraham Lincoln, but David hasn't made up his mind yet. I think I shall be a Spanish dancer."

They were beginning to look for costume materials in the closets and bureaus when a loud horn began to blow outside.

Mrs. Scott said. "Quickly, girls, it's an emergency! We must see if we can help. Amy, bring my medical supplies. Dear heaven, I hope it's not the boys!"

They rushed from the house toward the beach. Neighbors were running in the same direction.

They heard a man shouting, "WHALE! IT'S A BEACHED WHALE!"

As they reached the sand, they saw an enormous shape in the shallow water next to the beach. Coming closer, they could see that it really and truly was a whale, a huge, black whale. It was still alive. Sarah Elizabeth had seen whales from a distance, spouting in the ocean, but this great creature in front of her was beyond belief.

All of a sudden, some rough-looking boys began throwing rocks at the whale. They were aiming for its eyes. The whale looked straight at Sarah Elizabeth as if she could help. What could she do? If only someone could stop those boys.

Jason, where are you? she thought.

At that very moment, she heard a growling voice say, "TIME STAND STILL!" Jason stood before the whale.

The boys, with arms still raised, were motionless. Not a sound could be heard. The people stood as if they'd been turned to stone. Jason, with a smile at Sarah Elizabeth, began to pat and talk to the whale. The whale gave a great sigh and slowly blinked his eyes.

Then Jason T. Bear turned to face the ocean and raised his paws while chanting,

"Dolphins, waves and mermaid breath,
 Save this whale from certain death!"

As Jason lowered his paws, the waves grew larger. White egrets, gray pelicans and gray and white seagulls flew in three circles above the whale's head. A large number of dolphins gathered in the water opposite the whale. They hurled lines of seaweed to encircle the whale's tail. The wet sand beneath the whale began to slide toward the deeper part of the water. Then in two long lines, the dolphins swam, pulling the whale slowly out to the ocean. The whale sang a magnificent whale-song as it moved to safety.

Sarah Elizabeth hugged Jason who once more turned his attention to the people who were still standing like statues.

"TIME RETURN!" shouted Jason.

With a growl, he moved in front of the boys. They hung their heads in shame, dropping the rocks which were still clutched in their hands.

Jason spoke to them quietly. "Your hearts are changed forever. You will return to the city where you will help lost animals. The stagecoach leaves in five minutes. I will make the trip with you."

The townspeople were scratching their heads in wonder. How had the whale returned to the ocean? One moment it was in danger of death, and now they could see it spouting and singing far out on the waves. Who was that small, gray bear walking with the boys to the stagecoach stop?

Mrs. Scott and Amy caught up with George and David as they headed for home. They talked excitedly about what had happened at the beach. Rosie wagged her tail and barked to show her interest.

Sarah Elizabeth and Jessica walked behind the others.

"Sarah Elizabeth," said Jessica, "was Jason T. Bear there? I thought for a moment I saw him. Did he save the whale?"

"Yes, Jessica. Jason not only saved the whale, but also changed the lives of those boys forever."

As they came to the main street, the stagecoach dashed past them.

(If they'd looked at the lead horse, they would have seen Jason riding it bareback, or should I say bear back?)

CHAPTER 9
Teddy Talk

A few days after the whale rescue, the dolls were home alone. They were sitting on the porch sewing their costumes.

"Sarah Elizabeth, is Jason T. Bear a teddy bear?" asked Jessica.

"At first I thought so, but now I'm sure he's much more than a teddy, Jessica," said Sarah Elizabeth.

A breeze stirred the trees near the porch. The dolls looked up from their sewing to see Jason T. Bear sitting on the porch railing.

"Good afternoon, my dears. How are you this fine day?"

"Why Jason, we were just speaking of you. Jessica wondered if you were a real teddy bear. I told her I thought you were much more than that."

"How very wise of you, my dear." Jason stretched and ruffled his fur a bit. "I know I greatly resemble a teddy bear, but I have lived ever so much longer than teddy bears. Why, I even remember seeing the early dolls in Egypt thousands of years ago. In the beginning, I was told that I would be the Universal Bear. My mission in the world is to travel through time with a message of love and kindness for all who will listen. Does that make things clearer for you?"

"Yes, Jason. You seem to be doing your work beautifully," said Sarah Elizabeth.

"How is your visit going, Sarah Elizabeth?"

"It's perfect, Jason. Everyone has been very sweet to me. I will have so much to tell when I get home."

"I see that you are sewing costumes, my dears. For a party?"

"Yes, Mr. Bear, we are trying to finish them for the town's party tomorrow night," said Jessica. "Will you be able to come to it? Everyone would be happy to meet you."

"Very kind of you, my dear, and please call me Jason. I suppose I might be able to pop in for a little while. I would like to meet your family since Sarabeth and I will be leaving on the following day."

"Oh Sarah Elizabeth! You didn't tell me. Goodness gracious! Oh me, oh my! Ouch! Now I've pricked my finger for the tenth time today."

"Jessica, I really didn't know that I'd be leaving so soon," said Sarah Elizabeth, giving her a hug. "If Jason says it is time to go, he must have a good reason."

"Jason, will you comfort Jessica in some way? I think she will need a good friend when I leave. Amy is wonderful to her, but she'll be gone often now that school is starting."

Jason T. Bear had a gleam in his eye. "Sarabeth, I promise that Jessica will have a fine friend before you return to your home. Yes, yes, hum dee dum. Capital idea! I must leave now, but I will see you tomorrrrrrow..."

Jason T. Bear faded out of sight.

CHAPTER 10
An Enchanting Party

A huge, silvery moon cast its light upon the outdoor dance arena. Sounds of music and laughter filled the air, while myriads of shimmering fireflies whirled about the willow trees.

Off to the side, "Cleopatra" and a dainty princess dressed in pale blue watched the dancers.

"Sarah Eliz...I mean, Cleopatra, when do you think Jason will get here?"

"He should be here soon, Your Highness. It's nearly ten o'clock, and the party ends at midnight." Sarah Elizabeth smiled at Jessica.

Just at that moment Amy danced by, dressed all in pink velvet and lace.

"Look! There's Amy dancing with Shakespeare. Didn't her Juliet costume turn out well? Thank goodness we were able to finish David's King Neptune costume in time." Sarah Elizabeth sighed as she remembered the rush they had to finish his crown of seashells.

"All of the costumes are wonderful. Why don't we join the dancers while we're waiting, Sarah Elizabeth? I can hardly keep my feet still," said Jessica.

The dolls found an opening on the dance floor. Soon they, too, became a part of the night rainbow formed by the dancers in their colorful costumes, as they turned and circled beneath the moonlight.

After a few dances, the dolls decided to look for Jason again. As they were walking, they heard a familiar voice behind them.

"Forgive me, my dears, are you looking for someone?" Even behind mask and cape, it was obviously Jason T. Bear.

"We've been looking for you, Jason. What a beautiful purple cape!"

"Thank you, Sarabeth. It was given to me long ago, but that's a story I will save for another time," said Jason.

"Jessica, I have a great surprise for you. You must turn around three times, cup your hands and hold them out in front of you."

Jessica did so, giving Jason a puzzled look.

The bear waved his paw in the air, and a large yellow leaf began to fall from the tree above them. As it swirled slowly down, the dolls saw it change mid-air into a beautiful golden butterfly. Then it fluttered about near Jessica, settling into her hands. Jessica could hardly contain herself.

"Sarah Elizabeth, look! The butterfly is sitting in my hands." Just as she said this, the butterfly vanished, and in its place, was a sparkling gold and diamond ring.

"Oh my! It's Amy's ring! Jason, is it really her ring? Will it vanish like the butterfly? How did you...? I'm so happy, I could cry." Jessica hugged Sarah Elizabeth and Jason. Then she began to dance a very "un-princess-like" dance, kicking her heels in the air while laughing and hugging her friends in between hops and jumps.

"Slow down, Jessica, or you'll wear yourself out. Remember there are more surprises this evening." Jason T. Bear tried to look stern, but he was having a hard time holding back a chuckle.

"Take Sarabeth with you and bring the ring to Amy. I'll wait here for you."

The dolls gave Jason another hug and then dashed off to find Amy. It wasn't long before they found her resting on a bench.

"Amy! Look what I have for you." Jessica held out the ring.

"Jessica, where on earth did you find it?"

"I know this sounds strange, Amy, but tonight when Jason T. Bear arrived, he had me turn around three times. A big yellow leaf fell from a tree, turned into a butterfly which sat in my hands. The butterfly disappeared, and there was your ring."

"Jessica, you have a marvelous imagination. Now tell me who really gave it to you." Amy was smiling as she tried on her ring.

"I knew you wouldn't believe me," said Jessica looking hurt.

"Amy," said Sarah Elizabeth, "I was there when it happened. My friend, Jason, has magical powers. You should be happy that your ring is back."

"I truly am, Sarah Elizabeth. I'm sorry that I doubted you, Jessica, but you must admit that it was a very unusual way to find the ring. I will go and show it to Mama now, but please ask Jason to stay at the party so that I can thank him for his kindness."

CHAPTER 11
Blue Ribbons

When the dolls returned to Jason, they gave him Amy's message. He told them that he'd be very happy to meet her. Then he asked Jessica to sit on the bench under the willow tree, close her eyes and count slowly to ten. As Jessica did this, Jason gave a flourish with his cape, and there on the bench beside Jessica sat a handsome, brown teddy bear.

"Open your eyes, Jessica," said Jason.

Jessica did so and looked straight into the eyes of her new friend.

"This is Alexander, Jessica. He will never leave you and will protect you from all harm. In return, you must promise to give him tender loving care for all of his days. Please see that he has a proper honey supply and a fish dinner once a week. Since your garden has a fine supply of berries, Alexander should be quite content."

"How do you do, Jessica," said Alexander, smiling shyly.

"How do you do, Alexander? I'm very pleased to meet you."

"Jason, you are a marvel!" said Sarah Elizabeth, as she watched Jessica and Alexander talking together.

"Sarabeth, will you honor me with this dance?" asked Jason.

"I'd love to," said Sarah Elizabeth.

The doll and bear danced with such grace that the other dancers moved back in order to watch them. They had only been dancing a short time, when a man dressed as a pirate stepped forward on the stage.

"Attention everyone! It's time for the costume judging. Gentlemen, move to the left, ladies to the right. The judges will pass among you and then come to the stage where they will choose the winners."

The music began again, and the "pirate" invited everyone to dance once more. At exactly 11:30, the music stopped and the pirate called out in a loud voice, "THE WINNER OF THE GENTLEMEN'S AWARD IS KING NEPTUNE."

Sarah Elizabeth and Jessica looked at each other in wonder. The "last minute" costume had been a success. Many cheers greeted David as he received his blue ribbon and a huge basket filled with fruit, small cakes and other sweets.

As the pirate prepared to announce the winner of the lady's contest, Jason T. Bear nudged Alexander with his paw. He was trying to keep a straight face, but his nose was beginning to twitch.

The pirate began to say "LITTLE BO PEEP, PLEASE STEP FORWARD." He got as far as "LITTLE BO..." and taking another look at his card, said in a confused voice, "Uh, hmmm, sorry, WILL CLEOPATRA, QUEEN OF EGYPT, uh, WINNER OF THE LADIES' CONTEST, PLEASE COME FORWARD?"

Sarah Elizabeth looked at Jason, who gave her a push toward the stage. Jessica was laughing and clapping her hands. Sarah Elizabeth continued to look back at Jason, who gave her a wink. Her feet kept moving forward, so there was nothing she could do but climb the stairs to the platform.

The audience applauded wildly as a very small, but regal "Cleopatra" stood before them in her lovely gold and white gown. She was presented with a blue ribbon, a lovely silk scarf and a bouquet of red roses.

When Sarah Elizabeth opened her mouth to say that she didn't deserve the honor, the only words that came out were, "Thank you, dear people." She made her way back to Jason and began to question him.

"Pish tosh, Sarabeth. How could you think that I had anything to do with your win? Didn't you hear the applause? Didn't you see the smiling faces of the judges? You won fair and square."

(Now just in case you were wondering, Jason had been watching the crowd earlier at the party and noticed a young girl, who was dressed like a shepherdess. She was very pretty, but she was telling everyone that she'd win the costume contest. She said her daddy was important, and his friends would see to it that she won. Jason had decided she'd be wrong about that.)

"All right, Jason, but I'm still sure that another name was nearly announced." Then Sarah Elizabeth gave roses from her bouquet to Jessica, Jason and Alexander. "Jessica," she said, "let's find Mrs. Scott and Amy. I want to give them some roses, too. Come along with us, Jason and Alexander, so that they can meet you."

The bears followed the dolls toward the area in which many of the ladies were gathered.

"There they are!" cried Jessica. "Amy, Mrs. Scott, look who we have with us!" Jessica introduced the bears, and Sarah Elizabeth gave roses to Amy and her mother.

Amy thanked Jason for finding her ring and asked if he and Alexander could stay with them as their guests.

Everyone was sad to learn that Sarah Elizabeth and Jason were really leaving in the morning. However, when Jason said that Alexander would be staying with them permanently, Mrs. Scott, Amy and Jessica were smiling again.

Mrs. Scott asked Jason to stay overnight with them. He agreed, and then they all went to look for Mr. Scott and the boys. When they found them, Jason and Alexander were introduced to them. Since the dance was over, Mr. Scott said it was time to head for home. They said their "goodbyes" to friends and neighbors and walked up the hill to their home.

George, David and the bears decided to sleep on the porch since it was a warm and starry night. The others went to their rooms, and after getting ready for bed, were soon fast asleep.

Early in the morning, before the others were awake, Jason woke Sarah Elizabeth and told her that it was time to leave. He gave her a few moments to write a note:

Dear Scott Family,

I love you very much, but now I must leave with Jason. I will always remember you. Someday, we will meet again.

xoxo, Sarah Elizabeth

P.S. Alexander, please take good care of Jessica.

Jason T. Bear took Sarah Elizabeth's hand in his left paw as he began to rub his gold medal. He chanted slowly:

"Wings of gold and crystal bells,
Starlight in the night,
Take us swiftly through the years,
As we fade from sight."

CHAPTER 12
The Return

Sarah Elizabeth heard a loud purring. In the dark, she could see two sets of eyes - one pair of blue, one pair of gold – staring at her.

"Tuptim! Blackberry! What happened? I must be home!"

Sarah Elizabeth gave each cat a hug and a gentle rub behind their ears. The cats purred their pleasure at seeing her again. Then they looked toward the other side of the room. Sarah Elizabeth followed their gaze, and much to her delight, saw Kristi sleeping in her big brass bed.

"Kristi!" With a wild scramble, Sarah crossed the room and climbed up on the high bed in order to wake Kristi up and give her a hug and a kiss.

"Sarah Elizabeth!" Kristi woke with a start. "Thank heaven! I thought I'd never see you again. Where did you go?"

"I had a chance to Travel in Time, Kristi. I had to make up my mind right away. I thought everything would be all right if I left a note for the professors."

"We really thought you'd been kidnapped, Sarah Elizabeth. It just wasn't like you to go off like that."

"Oh dear, I'm so sorry you were worried, but you see, I rescued this marvelous bear. King Neptune had played a trick on him. Well anyway, Jason T. Bear asked if I'd like to travel back through Time with him. I told him I had to stay and keep Tuptim company. Then he magically gave us Blackberry, and I knew that everything would be all right.

"Kristi, it was amazing! We visited this very town in the year 1910. Everything was so different. There weren't any cars or telephones. They didn't have television, dishwashers, hot water or refrigerators. There were only a few homes on the hills, and there weren't any on the beach. There was a costume party, and I won a prize for my Cleopatra costume. Oh! I almost forgot! Jason rescued an enormous whale." Sarah Elizabeth finally took a breath at this point.

"Best of all, Kristi, I met a darling doll named Jessica, and her family turned out to be the professor's family. I met his father, his grandparents and his aunt and uncle. I even met their dog, Rosie."

When Sarah Elizabeth took another breath, Kristi said, "It sounds as if you've had some fantastic adventures. What does time-travel feel like Sarah Elizabeth? Do you feel as if you have jet-lag now? Was it really my father's family? Before I forget, Emily called and said that your book about teddy bears is waiting for you at the book shop. And speaking of bears, when do I get to meet your fabulous bear friend?"

"I'm glad Emily has my book, Kristi. To answer your questions, Jason should be here soon. You'll be crazy about him, and he'll love you. Yes, it really was your father's family. Time-travel is a breeze with Jason. You close your eyes, he says some magic words, and you find yourself in another time. I do feel tired, but I'm so happy to see you again. When do you have to go back to the university?"

"I have to leave tomorrow afternoon, Sarah Elizabeth. I hope Jason will be here before then. Good grief! It's only three in the morning. I thought it was nearly time to get up. We'd better get some sleep. Will you tell me more about your adventures in the morning?" Kristi gave her doll a sleepy hug and turned on her side.

"Good night, Kristi. We'll talk in the morning. I love you." Sarah Elizabeth climbed down from Kristi's bed and got into her own little bed. As she snuggled under the blankets, she remembered the costume party and the fun of being "Cleopatra" for an evening.

I'll have to ask Jason if he can take me to Ancient Egypt, she thought. *Maybe we could visit the real Cleopatra. I wonder if she was as beautiful and witty as the books say?*

Sarah Elizabeth fell fast asleep, dreaming of pyramids, camels and Egyptian dolls.

(Yes, there was Jason T. Bear, sitting in the pine tree underneath the moon. He was already making plans for a trip with Sarah Elizabeth to Ancient Egypt.)

Adventures in Egypt

CHAPTER 1
The Lost Kitten

Sarah Elizabeth shook her head as she looked around the garden. The doll watched some brightly-colored birds flying about the tall palm trees. They were very different from the birds in her own garden. She didn't recognize any of the beautiful flowers. And what was that lovely spicy fragrance in the air?

Sarah Elizabeth remembered going to sleep in her bed at home dreaming of pyramids, camels and Egyptian dolls. She still felt tired and a little dizzy, so she sat down on a large, smooth rock beside a pool of water. She tried to remember what had happened before she arrived in the garden. All she could think of was Jason T. Bear's magical words:

"Wings of gold and crystal bells,
Starlight in the night,
Take us swiftly through the years,
As we fade from sight."

The doll wished that Jason were with her to tell her where she was. She had a feeling that they had traveled through time again.

It was getting very warm in the garden. Sarah Elizabeth moved a little on the rock to get in the shade of a tree. Just as she did this, she heard a faint sound coming from the nearby bushes.

She listened carefully and heard it again. She moved closer to the bushes and very gently pulled the branches back.

There looking up at her, was the tiniest black kitten she'd ever seen. It shivered all over as she picked it up and began to comfort it. "There, there, little kitten, where's your mother? You're much too young to be here by yourself."

"Mew, mew," said the kitten, blinking its eyes.

"You're hungry aren't you, poor thing. There must be a house somewhere nearby. Let's see if we can find it and get some milk for you. If only you could tell me where your mother is."

The kitten licked Sarah Elizabeth's hand and began to purr. Still holding the kitten, the doll began walking along a path in the garden. She passed huge tree ferns near a splashing waterfall and was walking near a group of olive trees when she was suddenly grabbed roughly from behind.

Looking up, she saw four enormous men with spears towering over her. Sarah Elizabeth screamed and nearly dropped the kitten.

"Let go of me. Put me down. You're hurting me. Don't you dare hurt this kitten," the doll scolded.

The men shouted at her and pointed to the kitten. The tallest of the men snatched the kitten from her arms. The next thing she knew, she was thrown in a sack, and all was darkness.

CHAPTER 2
The Palace

After bouncing and jouncing in the dark for what seemed like hours, but may have only been minutes, Sarah Elizabeth felt the sack hit the ground. Someone opened it and pulled her out. She was unable to stand and sank trembling to the floor. Then as she looked about, her eyes grew large with both fear and wonder.

She was in a magnificent room. It was decorated with pillars of marble and carved furniture of the finest woods. There were beautiful designs painted on the ceiling and walls. Huge men holding feathered fans stood beside an enormous throne upon which sat a king in a golden robe and a high red hat. The room was filled with dark-haired men and women dressed in long gowns.

A young girl, sitting next to the king, held the little kitten Sarah Elizabeth had found. Seated next to the girl was a doll who was staring at Sarah Elizabeth.

The king was speaking, but Sarah Elizabeth couldn't understand a word he was saying. From time to time he would pause as if he wished her to answer him. As her head cleared, she decided to speak to him.

"Your Majesty, my name is Sarah Elizabeth. I am a doll from California. What have I done to be treated in this way?"

The king looked puzzled and spoke to a bald man standing near him. The man shook his head and glared at Sarah Elizabeth. Then she saw the doll whisper in the girl's ear. The girl touched the king's arm and spoke to him as he bent toward her. The king nodded his head. The girl said something to the doll, who began to speak.

"I am the Egyptian doll, Lanata. I belong to Cleopatra, daughter of King Ptolemy Auletes, The Flute Player. You are accused of kidnapping Saphira, Cleopatra's precious kitten. Not long ago, you would have been beheaded on the spot for such behavior. No one in Egypt has been allowed to harm a cat. How could you bring dishonor upon the dolls of the world by such an act? The king's advisors suggest that your stuffing be pulled slowly out of your body and that your outer covering be fed to goats."

At last Sarah Elizabeth could understand someone, but she was shocked by Lanata's words. This must be ancient Egypt. The young girl was Cleopatra. And she, Sarah Elizabeth, was being unjustly accused of a crime for which she was innocent.

Sarah Elizabeth tried to smooth the wrinkles from her dress as she stood up. "Lanata, please tell the king and his daughter that I found the kitten crying beneath a bush near a pond of floating flowers. I was trying to rescue it and find some milk for it. I love all animals, especially kittens, and would never do anything to harm them."

Lanata looked more kindly at her and spoke to Cleopatra and the king. Just then an evil-looking man stepped forward shouting many words as he gestured wildly at Sarah Elizabeth. When he had finished, Lanata told Sarah Elizabeth that he'd said the following:

"Great King Auletes, this intruder lies! I, Pothinus, have learned from the goddess, Bast, that this wicked female was stealing the kitten to hold it for ransom. In the name of the people of Egypt, I demand her death."

Lanata and Cleopatra whispered to each other. Then Cleopatra spoke to the court. When she finished, she clapped her hands twice. Lanata told Sarah Elizabeth that Cleopatra had sent for the Sacred White Cat, who was the earthly representative of Bast. "If you have spoken the truth, Sarah Elizabeth, you will have nothing to fear," said Lanata.

Her words made Sarah Elizabeth feel much better. However, she couldn't understand why Jason hadn't arrived to help her.

(If she'd looked high up on a nearby slender pillar, she might have seen a familiar furry friend.)

CHAPTER 3
The Sacred White Cat

The silvery sound of tiny bells began to fill the Great Hall. A very small man with a very large, round head entered. He was carrying a golden container from which strongly scented smoke was rising. Lanata whispered to Sarah Elizabeth that this was Madrian, Cleopatra's most trusted assistant.

Next came six young girls walking into the room in single file scattering pink rose petals. They were followed by ten young boys holding black marble statues of cats. Then as the bells stilled, four young men stepped into the room bearing an ebony and ivory platform upon which sat a very beautiful and very old white cat.

Cleopatra bowed to the Sacred Cat as did all of those who were present. Then she spoke to the cat while Lanata translated her words to Sarah Elizabeth.

"Oh Sacred Cat, the foreign doll, Sarah Elizabeth, has been accused of kidnapping my kitten, Saphira. The doll says that she was trying to help Saphira. Would you, in all your wisdom, consider this matter and help us see the truth?"

Then Cleopatra placed her kitten on the pillow next to the Sacred White Cat. Madrian handed her the golden container, and Cleopatra swung it by its chain as she walked three times around the cat's platform. Sarah Elizabeth wanted to cough from the strange smoke which was filling the room, but she managed to keep from doing so.

The Sacred White Cat licked the kitten's ears. Then she stared at Cleopatra, who snapped her fingers at the young men, causing them to lower the platform to the ground. The Sacred White Cat stepped from the platform and walked slowly over to where Sarah Elizabeth now sat. There was a hush throughout the room. The cat stood before Sarah Elizabeth and circled her, rubbing against her and purring loudly. She sniffed Sarah Elizabeth's nose and gave her a look of love and sympathy. Then she walked back to the platform, picked Saphira up gently by the back of the neck, carried her to the doll and placed her in her lap.

At this, the king began to play his flute, and Lanata and Sarah Elizabeth smiled at each other. The only frowning faces in the court belonged to the two advisors who had tried to harm Sarah Elizabeth.

The Sacred White Cat returned to her platform and was carried out of the room by her attendants.

Sarah Elizabeth stood up holding the tiny kitten and brought her to Cleopatra. Taking the kitten, Cleopatra spoke to Sarah Elizabeth as Lanata translated, "The Sacred White Cat is never wrong. You, Sarah Elizabeth, spoke the truth and have won our friendship. We apologize to you for our terrible mistake and for the mistreatment you received at the hands of the king's guards. We hope that you will forgive us and remain our most honored guest for as long as you wish. You must be hungry and tired so we will attend to those matters first."

Cleopatra spoke to a tall young woman standing near her. The woman came to Sarah Elizabeth and taking her by the hand, led her, with Lanata following, out of the Great Hall.

CHAPTER 4
Jason's Arrival

Sarah Elizabeth was given a thorough cleaning. Her soiled dress, pinafore and ribbon were removed, and she was dressed in an Egyptian gown of lovely material. As she was being cleaned, the doll learned that the young woman helping her was Charmian, Cleopatra's lady-in-waiting.

A little later, another young woman arrived with a tray filled with honeyed cakes and fruits. Lanata said that this was Iras, another favorite attendant of Cleopatra's. As Sarah Elizabeth was about to bite into a small golden cake that was simply oozing with honey, she heard a familiar, low growly voice coming from behind her right shoulder.

"Mmmmmmm, Sarah Elizabeth, so good to see you, my dear. You look quite fetching in your new gown. Mmmmmmm, if my nose does not deceive me, I believe you are about to have an Egyptian honey cake. Mmmmmmm. Honey cake. Ah yes, it brings back such sweet memories…"

"JASON T. BEAR! It's about time you were here. Where have you been? I nearly had my stuffing pulled out of my body. I might have been fed to the goats. Everyone thought I'd stolen Cleopatra's kitten. If it hadn't been for the Sacred White Cat…"

"Now, now, Sarabeth, I would have rescued you if you had been in real danger, but I knew that things were going to be all right once the Sacred White Cat arrived. I knew she would see

50

the truth of the matter. By the way, she wants me to bring you to her for an informal visit after you have had a good night's sleep. Urrr, ahem, would you happen to have an extra honey cake for a certain hungry bear, Sarabeth? And I would be very pleased to meet your new friends."

Sarah Elizabeth blushed as she realized that she hadn't introduced Jason, nor had she offered him any of the honey cakes. "Of course, Jason, I'm sorry I didn't think to offer you one. Maybe my head is still rattled from that awful ride in the sack." Sarah Elizabeth passed the plate of cakes to Jason. Then she introduced him to Charmian and Iras who were fascinated by the furry newcomer.

As Jason busied himself with a honey cake, Sarah Elizabeth told him that she would appreciate it very much if he would help her both to understand and to be understood by the Egyptians.

Jason produced a velvet bag and said, "No problem, Sarabeth, I have a very special amulet for you. If you will put on this scarab bracelet, your wish will be granted." Jason pulled a silver bracelet with a strange beetle-shaped stone out of the bag and handed it to her.

Sarah Elizabeth was just putting on the bracelet when Cleopatra entered the room holding Saphira. Cleopatra's beautiful eyes widened when she saw Jason. She turned quickly to Lanata. "Do my eyes deceive me or is that hairy person a bear? I have seen pictures of such creatures in our library."

"Yes, Cleopatra, he is the good friend of Sarah Elizabeth and the Sacred White Cat. Evidently he is a fur-person of some importance."

Sarah Elizabeth was delighted to find that she could understand every word spoken by Cleopatra to Lanata. The bracelet was working. She stood up and taking Jason's paw, led him over to Cleopatra. "Your Royal Highness, I would like to present my very good friend, Jason T. Bear, Time-Traveler."

Jason bowed a most elegant bow. "At your service, Your Royal Highness, I am delighted to meet you. I have known many of your noble ancestors in the past."

Cleopatra's eyes sparkled with delight as she said, "This is turning out to be a very interesting day. At first, I thought it would be quite boring, but it has been full of surprises and good company. Something tells me that you, Jason T. Bear, are filled with goodness. Perhaps, during your visit with us, you will let a bit of it rub off on some of my relatives. Will you be able to stay long enough for my father's birthday party? We will have many fine fish dishes and a large supply of honey. It is my understanding that bears especially enjoy fish and honey."

"I would be most pleased to attend your father's party. I would do so even without the added enjoyment of fish and honey. Now if you will forgive me, Your Highness, I must look in on the Sacred White Cat before the sun goes down."

"Just how well do you know the Sacred White Cat, Jason?" asked Cleopatra.

"Very well indeed, Your Highness, we have been friends for many a century. She is most remarkable. Yes, most remarkable." Jason bowed to Cleopatra and disappeared.

Cleopatra, looking thoughtful, repeated his words, "Most remarkable." Then turning to Sarah Elizabeth, she said, "My little friend, someday, you must tell me how it is that we can finally understand each other, but right now it is time for you to get some sleep. In the morning, you will visit the Sacred White Cat, and then you will have a tour of our wonderful country. You will need to be rested so that you can fully enjoy the sights. Iras and Lanata will attend you. Pleasant dreams." Cleopatra smiled as she, Saphira and Charmian left the room.

CHAPTER 5
A Visit with Aunt Fluffy

It was still early in the morning when Jason and Sarah Elizabeth arrived at the Temple of the Sacred White Cat. A servant led them past gold and jeweled statues of cats to a chamber in which they found the Sacred White Cat lying on a blue silk pillow in a large woven basket.

Her eyes were closed, but as they came near, she opened them and said in a sweet but slightly scratchy voice, "Good morning, dear friends. Please pull up some pillows and sit down."

Sarah Elizabeth was delighted to find that with her bracelet she could now understand the language of cat.

As Jason brought two pillows closer to the cat, he said, "We're so glad you have allowed us this visit, Fluffy, I mean, Oh Sacred One, urrr, just a slip of the tongue, but no harm done, I hope." Jason looked embarrassed.

"Now Jason, it's been too many years and too many mice in the cupboard, for you to put on airs with me. You've known me since I was a young cat, before my sacred days, so 'Fluffy' is just fine with me. As for you, my dear," she said as she smiled at Sarah Elizabeth, "you may call me Aunt Fluffy. I hear you will be touring our country soon. Is that true?"

"Yes, Aunt Fluffy, Cleopatra says we will sail on the Nile River to visit the pyramids and the Sphinx."

"Lovely, my dear, how well I remember the Nile trip on the royal barge. It's been a long, long time since I've visited the Sphinx. I used to see him at least once a year. Sometimes the Pharaoh took me on the river to go fishing, but that was many years ago. These days, I don't feel like leaving my favorite pillow for more than a few hours at a time." The cat's eyes closed, and for a moment, Sarah Elizabeth thought she'd fallen asleep. Then the cat opened her eyes and said, "Ah yes, my dears, where was I?"

"Fishing with the Pharaoh, Fluffy. I certainly wish I could have been on one of those trips. Those Nile fish must have been delicious," said Jason.

"That reminds me, Jason, did you tell Sarah Elizabeth how you and I first met?"

"No, Fluffy, why don't you tell her?"

"Would you like to hear my story, Sarah Elizabeth?"

"Oh yes, Aunt Fluffy. I'd love to hear it."

The white cat adjusted her tail and paws and then began. "When I was born, everyone except my mother was horrified. I didn't look at all like the sleek, dark, short-haired Egyptian cats. I was white, long-haired and exceedingly round. My mother told me that I was pretty in an unusual way. It was hard for me to believe her though when the other cats called me names like: Roly-Poly, Chunky, Powder-Puff, and Fur-Ball.

"One day, I had crawled into my favorite hiding place in one of the smallest rooms in the palace. I was crying and feeling very sorry for myself. I had decided to cut and dye my long white hair. All of a sudden this marvelous, furry fellow appeared and introduced himself. Yes, it was Jason T. Bear." The white cat smiled at Sarah Elizabeth.

"Jason said that I was lucky to be different. Since I was the only long-haired, round white cat in the country, I could never be lost for long. He said that my long hair would keep me warm in winter and cool in summer. It would make it hard for another cat to scratch or bite me. Jason thought that my roundness was more pleasing to look at than the boniness of some of the other cats. After he told me those reasons and a few others which I have forgotten, I began to think of myself in a very different way. I carried my head and tail much higher when I walked, and I felt so much better about myself." The cat's voice had been getting scratchier as she spoke, and she asked Jason to go on with her story.

Jason got up from his pillow and began to walk back and forth as he talked. "The day after our meeting, Fluffy was brought before the young king. He had heard of the unusual cat and wanted to see her for himself. The king thought she was beautiful. He consulted his advisors and the temple priests and within the week, Fluffy had become the Sacred White Cat of Egypt. There were celebrations in her honor. Artists were set to work making statues and paintings of Fluffy. Wherever she went, crowds cheered and threw flowers in her path. All of this might have turned the head of another cat, but Fluffy has never taken advantage of her fame. She is very wise, and she can always see into the hearts of those who come before her."

"Thank you, dear Jason, for all of your kind words. Now Sarah Elizabeth, I would like to hear about the cats in your country."

"Your story is so inspiring, Aunt Fluffy. No wonder you were so understanding and kind with me. As for the cats in my country, they are of every size, shape and color. I've seen many long-haired white cats, although none are as lovely as you. In my own family there are two cats. One is a very plump Siamese cat with beige and dark-brown hair and blue eyes. The other cat is small with black hair and golden eyes. Jason gave us the black cat, but that's another story.

"Many people in my country love and take good care of their cats. However, thousands and thousands of cats and kittens are unwanted, and they die each year. It is a terrible problem."

The Sacred White Cat's eyes looked sad as she said, "Sarah Elizabeth, my heart is heavy to hear this. Perhaps your country needs to pass new laws protecting the cats. In the meantime, you and your family and friends will have to teach by your good example. Oh my, I'm getting very sleepy. You'll have to forgive me, my dears. I think it must be my naptime. I've enjoyed your visit so much. Would you give my ears a bit of a scratch before you go? Ah, that's perfect." The cat began to purr contentedly.

"Goodbye, Aunt Fluffy. Thank you for sharing your story with me," said Sarah Elizabeth.

"Sweet dreams, Fluffy. May they be filled with mice and cream," said Jason.

"Goodbye, my dears." The Sacred White Cat closed her eyes and was fast asleep before they left her chamber.

CHAPTER 6
The Pyramids

The days were going by so quickly. Sarah Elizabeth pinched herself. Was she really sailing on the Nile heading toward the pyramids? Cleopatra had said this morning that they would reach them by afternoon. Sarah Elizabeth thought of the book she had read several years ago. It said that the Great Pyramid was the largest pyramid in the world, but she had forgotten how tall it was. She always did have trouble remembering numbers.

This trip had been fun already. Madrian had come along at the last minute to be their tour guide. He kept everyone laughing at his funny comments. It wasn't just his remarks; it was the way in which he said them. He had the habit of raising one eyebrow and tilting his head to the side that reminded Sarah Elizabeth of a wise little bird.

Cleopatra had said that the ride on the royal barge might be a bit tiring for everyone, and that they would have to "rough it" on the trip. So far they had enjoyed soft pillows, delicious food, musical entertainment and perfect weather. Maybe for Cleopatra "roughing it" meant missing her daily milk bath.

Just as Sarah Elizabeth was thinking this, Madrian gave a shout, "Peacock feathers! We're almost there. Put on your sandals everyone. Take your seats. Hold on to your pillows, your wigs and your jewelry. Last one off the barge gets eaten by a crocodile."

"Crocodile?" Sarah Elizabeth looked at Lanata. "Madrian is kidding, isn't he?"

"Of course, Sarah Elizabeth, I've never seen one around here. They have other favorite places along the river."

Sarah Elizabeth was glad she hadn't known enough to worry about them earlier on the trip.

Before long, Cleopatra and her touring party had arrived at the edge of the desert, where they all gazed in awe at the enormous pyramids. Even Madrian was silent for a few moments.

Cleopatra was the first to speak. "I always have the strangest feeling when I am here. It is as if the Great Kings are watching me. Sarah Elizabeth, what do you think of this place?"

"It's amazing, Your Highness. The pictures I've seen have never done justice to the pyramids. There's something strange here, too. My head feels light, and I keep thinking that someone wishes to talk to me."

"Oh, that's probably the Sphinx," said Madrian. "He's always looking for someone to talk with, but first let me tell you about the Great Pyramid. It was built for King Cheops, also known as King Khufu. It's 481 feet tall, made of over two million stone blocks, each weighing 5,000 pounds. It took twenty years to build it, and every man in Egypt had to work on it for several months a year."

"Excuse me, Madrian, but I remember being told that its base was large enough to hold ten football fields," said Sarah Elizabeth.

"What kind of fields?" asked Madrian.

"Oh, I forgot that you wouldn't know football. It's a game that's very popular in my country. Two teams of men play with a ball on a large field. Each team tries to get the ball past the other team to the end of the field by throwing, carrying or kicking it."

"Football, hmmm, you'll have to tell me more about this. I love games just as long as I get to win."

Cleopatra laughed. "You always win, Madrian. Someday we are going to find out your secret. Not that we think you cheat, but your good luck is hard to believe."

"It's skill, Your Highness, superior skill with just a bit of luck thrown in for good measure. It's all in the know-how, the right move, the best timing."

"All right, my superior little man, now will you please take us inside the Great Pyramid?"

"With pleasure, Your Highness. The mystical ceremonies are over for the month, making it possible for us to see more of the pyramid than usual. I will select two of your guards and a torch-bearer to go with us."

Lanata had turned a shade of pale green as Madrian was speaking.

"What's the matter, Lanata?" asked Sarah Elizabeth.

"I think I'd better wait outside. I was very queasy the last time I went on the tour."

"Iras will keep you company, Lanata," said Cleopatra. "She doesn't like the passageways either. Do you have a problem with long, dark, narrow places, Sarah Elizabeth?"

"Oh no, Your Highness. I wouldn't miss this tour for anything."

"Very well then, we will enter as soon as Madrian is ready."

CHAPTER 7
Within the Great Pyramid

The passageway within the pyramid was darker than night itself. No moon. No stars. The flames of the torch cast strange shadows on the walls.

Madrian was in his glory as he ordered the torch-bearer to shine light upon the designs and pictures which were painted on the ceilings and walls. "These are ancient picture-writings which warn intruders and thieves to beware," he said. "The false doors over there are to confuse robbers. Our walk will take us down to the Chamber of Chaos. Keep your hands at your sides and promise not to panic if we run into a snake or two. Suja, the Sacred Cobra, helps guard the pyramid and may be moving about at any level."

Sarah Elizabeth began to have second thoughts about the tour, but she knew it was too late to turn back. Snakes? She wished she had on hiking boots instead of sandals. Well, so far so good, nothing slithery.

Madrian was still talking, rarely taking a breath. "Yes, this pyramid was built at the exact center of the land surface of the entire earth. Most pyramids were burial places for the pharaohs, but not this one. It is a ceremonial pyramid. We are about to enter the lowest chamber. Follow me closely. If you look around the room, you will see painted scenes on the walls which represent the Underworld. Ooooof! Whazzat?"

There was a great flapping of wings as something flew past them. Everyone ducked down to let it fly by.

Cleopatra was the first to speak. "What on earth was that, Madrian? A bat?"

"Too large for a bat, Your Highness. It was probably Horus."

"Who's Horus?" asked Sarah Elizabeth.

"Horus, son of Osiris and Isis, is the king of the gods and the world. Sometimes he appears as a falcon. He may be trying to warn us of an unknown danger." Madrian motioned toward the door. "We'd better start upwards toward the Queen's Chamber."

They had only been walking for a few minutes when Sarah Elizabeth felt something slide past her feet. She was startled and jumped to the side, causing everyone to stop to see what was wrong.

"What's the matter, Sarah Elizabeth?" asked Cleopatra, turning to help her.

"Something very large moved near my feet and scared me. Did you feel it, too?"

"No, I haven't felt anything. Have you, Charmian?"

"No, Your Highness, but I thought I heard an odd noise."

The group started to move on but came to an abrupt stop as an enormous shadow of a cobra appeared on the wall. The guards quickly jumped in front of Cleopatra with their swords drawn. Charmian screamed and clutched at Sarah Elizabeth. The torchbearer was backing up and in danger of tripping over Madrian who was trying to see around the guards' legs.

"Hith!"

"What did you say, Madrian?"

"Nothing, Sweet Princess, I didn't say anything at all."

"Hith! Hith!"

"Charmian, is that you sneezing?" Cleopatra's voice was getting an edge to it.

Elizabeth Wright

"Look down here, Your Highneth. It'th Thujah, the Thacred Athp. Don't you recognithe me? I gueth I thould thay Thacred Cobra. Athp and Thnake are too hard for me to thay." The voice cracked and there was a loud sob. "I thought thingth were getting back to normal when I wath able to thcare all of you, but if you are only afraid of my thadow, I'll probably looth my job." The snake began to weep.

As the guards put their weapons away and moved aside, trying hard not to laugh, Sarah Elizabeth finally saw the Sacred Cobra. Its head was bowed, and it was shaking all over as it wept.

Cleopatra bent toward it. "There, there, Suja. I know you now. What has happened to your voice? You seem to be having trouble with your s's."

Suja looked up at Cleopatra. "Oh Great Printheth of the Nile, it all happened when I got angry at Thoth, the god of thpeech. I told him that he had a thilly name becauth of the 'th' thounth. From then on, I couldn't thay 'eth.' It'th been two weekth, and I don't know what to do." Suja began to cry again.

"Thuja, I mean Suja, I will speak to Thoth. He may forgive you if I tell him you will never make fun of his name again."

"Would you, Your Highneth? I really am thorry. Tell him I promith not to teathe him anymore. Will you thpeak to him thoon?"

"Tonight, Suja, when the moon is full, and we are on the Nile. I am sure he will listen to me."

"Thank you, Dear Printheth. May I athk another favor?"

"What is it, Sujah?"

"May I come with you on your tour? No one hath to be afraid of me. I couldn't thpit if I tried. When I lotht my 'eth,' I lotht my thpit, too."

Sarah Elizabeth remembered that cobras spit poison into their victims' eyes. She was sorry about Sujah's speech problem, but she really didn't mind that he couldn't spit poison now.

"Sujah, we'd be happy to have you join us," said Cleopatra. "You can slide along by my side. Madrian, we'd better move along quickly or we won't have time to see the Sphinx."

During the long climb upward, Madrian told one story after another about the ancient queens and kings of Egypt. The names were wonderful: Nefertiti, Akhenaten, Yuya, Tuya, Tiye, Amenhotep, Tutankhamun, and Ramesses. However his favorite stories were about Seneb the Dwarf who was a famous court tutor in the Old Kingdom. Seneb was one of Madrian's ancestors.

When they reached the Queen's Chamber, everyone, except Madrian was out of breath and in need of a rest. Madrian took advantage of this to give them another talk about King Cheops and the Great Pyramid.

"Madrian," said Cleopatra, "we praise your vast knowledge, but we've learned enough for the day. Our brains and bodies need a rest. Will you take us 'quietly' back in a few minutes?"

"Forgive me, Your Highness, if I've been too long-winded. I get excited when I have a chance to tell Egypt's history. The King's Chamber and the Grand Gallery are closed to us, so there's nothing left to see. The walk back will be easier as it's downhill all the way."

"Your Highneth," said Sujah, "I will thtay here if that'th all right with you. Will you remember to thpeak to Thoth for me?"

"You have my word, Sujah, but you must promise to watch your tongue from now on."

"Yeth, Divine Printheth I will be a much thmarter thnake in the future. Farewell everyone."

The Sacred Cobra curled itself up near the door as the group moved on down the long passageway which led to the outside.

CHAPTER 8
Meeting the Sphinx

After Cleopatra and her friends and attendants had left the Great Pyramid, they had moved on to see the Sphinx. Sarah Elizabeth and Madrian were standing, talking together.

"Madrian, how do you remember all of the history of Egypt?" asked Sarah Elizabeth.

"When you are born with a big head and a small body, your head has to work overtime," said Madrian laughing.

"DID SOMEONE SAY BIG HEAD? I HAVE A BIG HEAD AS WELL AS A BIG BODY," boomed a tremendous voice. "AND BEFORE YOU SAY ANYTHING ABOUT MY BODY, LITTLE MAN, I'M QUITE PLEASED WITH IT. IF I HAVE TO LIE ON THE DESERT FOR THOUSANDS OF YEARS, A LION'S SHAPE IS THE BEST FOR ME. YES, I CAN THINK WITH MY MAN'S HEAD AND REST COMFORTABLY WITH MY LION'S BODY. IT'S AN EXCELLENT COMBINATION."

"Hold on there, Your Sphinxness, I was speaking of myself when I said, 'Big Head.' There's no need to be defensive. Don't you remember me? We traded jokes and wisdom a few summers ago. I'm Madrian, Cleopatra's loyal assistant."

Madrian was tipping his head back so far in order to look up at the huge Sphinx that Sarah Elizabeth was certain he'd fall over backwards.

"MADRIAN, IS IT? WELL, WELL, FORGIVE ME, LITTLE FELLOW. OF COURSE I REMEMBER YOU. I MUST BE GETTING TOO SENSITIVE. THAT LAST GROUP OF TOURISTS GAVE ME A BAD TIME, AND SOMETHING HAS BEEN TICKLING MY EAR TODAY. YOU KNOW IT'S A REAL BURDEN NOT BEING ABLE TO SCRATCH."

As the Sphinx said this, Sarah Elizabeth heard a familiar voice shouting from above, "Helloooo down there! I'm up here in the ear of the Sphinx. Can you see me?"

"By the heavenly white lotus, who's that?" asked Cleopatra, who had just moved over near Sarah Elizabeth and Madrian to see what was going on.

"It's Jason T. Bear, Your Highness. I wonder how he'll get down from there?" said Sarah Elizabeth.

"He got up there, didn't he?" said Cleopatra. "Don't forget that what goes up, must come down."

"WHO'S IN MY EAR? I HEARD THAT!"

"It's your old friend, Jason T. Bear, in the shade of your ear. My paws were getting too hot walking on your barren desert. Terribly sorry, old chap, if my fur is tickling you. I would have said something sooner, but I thought you were taking a nap."

"JASON T. BEAR? HOLY HIPPOPOTAMUS! I SHOULD HAVE GUESSED THAT IT WAS YOU, BUT IT HAS BEEN ABOUT THREE HUNDRED YEARS SINCE YOUR LAST VISIT. IF I RECALL, YOU WERE WITH ALEXANDER THE GREAT."

"Absolutely correct, old friend. Alexander, it was. Ah! Those were rip-snorting days. Say, before I forget, the Sacred White Cat sends you greetings and apologizes for not visiting you lately. She's becoming a bit of a 'stay-at-home'."

"BY ALL MEANS, TELL THE SACRED WHITE CAT THAT I SEND HER MY BEST WISHES. SHE REALLY

SHOULD HAVE ANOTHER TRIP ON THE RIVER. IT WOULD BE JUST WHAT SHE NEEDS. TELL HER I ADVISED THAT."

"Certainly, old chum. Now I've got good news for you. I'm about to join the group on the ground. No more tickling of your ear."

Sarah Elizabeth was still looking upward, wondering if Jason would climb or roll down the Sphinx, when she felt a soft paw touch her shoulder. "Jason! I was worrying about how you'd get down, and here you are."

"Sorry if I startled you, Sarabeth. Have you been enjoying your tour? I had hoped to take the sailing trip with you but business detained me."

"It's been fantastic, Jason. Do you think you'll be able to go back with us?"

Before Jason could answer, the Sphinx called out, "CLEOPATRA! WHERE IS THE YOUNG PRINCESS? I HAVE AN IMPORTANT MESSAGE FOR HER."

"Here I am, Great Sphinx, standing near your left paw." Cleopatra waved her jeweled hand in the air.

"AH! NOW I SEE YOU, OR AT LEAST I SEE YOUR EMERALDS FLASHING. YOUR SISTER, BERENICE, WISHES YOU HARM, YOUNG PRINCESS. HER SMILES WILL HIDE HER EVIL INTENTIONS. BEWARE OF THE SILVER GOBLET."

"Your words will be remembered, Great Sphinx. No silver goblet will touch my lips from this day forward. As for Berenice, I will see behind her smiles."

"YOU ARE WISE, YOUNG PRINCESS. YOU WILL LIVE TO BE QUEEN OF EGYPT. YOU HAVE CHOSEN YOUR FRIENDS WELL. ALL WHO ARE WITH YOU THIS DAY

MAY BE TRUSTED. NOW, I WISH A FINAL WORD WITH MY OLD FRIEND, THE EAR-TICKLER."

Jason jumped up waving his paws. "Here I am, my friend."

"JASON, YOU MUST PROTECT YOUR YOUNG FRIEND, SARAH ELIZABETH. SHE HAS BEEN MARKED FOR DANGER, TOO. IF YOU AND MADRIAN JOIN FORCES, YOU CAN DEFEND BOTH CLEOPATRA AND SARAH ELIZABETH FROM TROUBLE."

"Thank you, old boy. I will be ever watchful. Even if unseen, I will be at their sides." Jason looked very serious as he spoke these words.

"Farewell for now, Great Sphinx," said Cleopatra. "Come, my trusted ones. We must return to the palace. I have never been one to run from danger. We will all be on guard. You have heard the name of my enemy."

CHAPTER 9
Preparing for the Banquet

Two days had passed since the trip on the Nile. Lanata and Sarah Elizabeth were sitting in Cleopatra's beautiful chamber. They had been asked to entertain Saphira while Iras and Charmian prepared Cleopatra for the king's birthday banquet. Cleopatra had already had her milk bath in the huge marble bathtub. It had been a struggle, but the dolls had kept the kitten from falling into it.

After Cleopatra's bath, her skin had been gently rubbed with precious oils. Her fingernails and toenails had been colored with red henna juice. Her lips were reddened and her eyes were lined with green and black kohl. Usually, Cleopatra's clothing was quite simple, but for this occasion, she was dressed in a gown of silver cloth. It reminded Sarah Elizabeth of stardust.

Iras had taken the loveliest royal blue sapphires from an ebony chest and was carefully securing them in Cleopatra's hair.

"Ouch! Iras, that hurts. Are you nearly finished? I should have worn my wig. Sometimes being a princess is such a pain."

"There, Sweet Mistress, the last jewel is in place," said Iras, holding up a metal mirror. "See how enchanting you look. Who would think that you were a little roughneck a year ago? With your scraped knees and messy hair, it didn't seem possible that you would ever be a dignified princess."

"Sometimes I miss those days, Iras. There were so few worries when I could run through the gardens playing ball and climbing trees."

"Speaking of playing, Your Highness, look at Saphira," said Sarah Elizabeth. The kitten had climbed into a large vase and was peeking over its edge.

Cleopatra laughed and said, "Charmian, bring the golden bowl to me."

Charmian did so, and Cleopatra took two lovely collars made from fresh flowers out of the bowl. One she placed about Lanata's neck and the other around Sarah Elizabeth's.

"Iras, please hand me my perfume."

Iras quickly handed a turquoise bottle to Cleopatra who put a little of the heavenly scent on the dolls' wrists. The dolls were delighted and thanked Cleopatra for the flowers and perfume.

Cleopatra picked up a narrow wooden case from a nearby table. "This is the gift I have for my father. I think it will make him happy." She opened the box and took an ancient bronze flute out of it. "It has taken me many months to find this flute. It is very rare and has a beautiful tone."

"It's a fabulous flute, Cleopatra. The king will be thrilled. I hope he will like my gift, too." Lanata took a tiny bottle shaped like a lion from a small bag and showed it to them.

"Your Highness," said Sarah Elizabeth, "that's such an unusual flute. Your father should be very pleased. He will love your gift, too, Lanata. I wish I had known it was the king's birthday, sooner. I could have brought him a gift from California. Do you suppose he'd like a flower from my collar?"

"What a perfect idea, Sarah Elizabeth. My father will love a flower from you. By the way, I would like it very much if you would just call me Cleopatra. I think of you as a dear friend now and would be happy to give you that privilege. If everyone is ready, we should go to the Dining Hall. Don't forget your gifts."

Gathering up her little kitten, Cleopatra moved gracefully out of the room followed by the dolls and her ladies-in-waiting.

CHAPTER 10
The Banquet

The royal cooks had been preparing a fabulous feast for days. They had been baking, boiling, chopping, cutting, dicing draining, grating, melting, mincing, paring, peeling, roasting, scrubbing, shredding, slicing, spicing, steaming, stewing, stuffing and tasting until they were ready to fall on their faces.

Now the enormous Dining Hall was filling with the nobility of Egypt and ambassadors from foreign countries. As Cleopatra in her silver gown entered the room, followed by the dolls and her ladies-in-waiting, all eyes were upon her. She seated herself on one of the golden lounge chairs and motioned the others to sit nearby.

Sarah Elizabeth sat down and began to look around the room admiring the marble pillars, the ivory tables, the golden dishes and most of all, the guests in the unusual costumes of their countries. As she looked about, her attention was caught by a young woman sitting near the king's advisor, Pothinus. The woman was staring at Cleopatra with an evil look in her eyes.

"Well, well, Cleopatra, this is the first time you have been on time for Father's birthday. I wonder how you managed to break your bad habit?" Her mouth smiled, but her eyes did not.

"Dear Berenice," Cleopatra replied, "what a charmer you are. You always say such sweet things to me. Are you not feeling well this evening, dear sister? You look rather ill. Perhaps it's the color of your makeup."

Berenice sputtered under her breath and glared at Cleopatra, who had turned away from her.

Sarah Elizabeth looked at Lanata with a question in her eyes.

"That's Cleopatra's sister, Berenice," whispered Lanata. "She's the one the Sphinx warned us about. Be on your guard."

"Cleopatra seems more than a match for her," said Sarah Elizabeth.

"She is, but Berenice will do anything to keep Cleopatra from becoming the queen." Just as Lanata was saying this, a drum began to beat and the king swept into the room accompanied by his fan-bearers and musicians. As soon as he was seated, each guest was presented with a flowered crown.

Then the servants began to bring in trays of food. There were countless varieties of meat, poultry and fish, huge platters of colorful vegetables, baskets of bread, bowls piled high with melons, pomegranates, grapes, figs, dates and berries. Each tray was a work of art decorated with leaves and flowers. Sarah Elizabeth wanted to try a taste of everything. She loved the unusual spices in the foods.

Jason T. Bear, wearing an Egyptian headdress, arrived as the first fish course was served. His timing was excellent since fish was one of his favorite foods. Saphira, the kitten, looked equally interested.

"Jason, I'm so glad you are here. I've seen Cleopatra's sister, Berenice. She's sitting over there in a pale green gown. Do you see how she stares at Cleopatra?"

"Don't fret, Sarabeth, I'm keeping an eye on her. Madrian and I are ready for any of her tricks. Ah, what a delicious dish of fish! Just the food to keep me alert! Sharpens the brain, you know."

At that moment, the music in the room grew louder, and a beautiful dancer whirled past them. She was dressed in a gown of many shades of blue. She wore bracelets of bells on her wrists and ankles. She looked like a gorgeous wild bird as she danced to the music of cymbals, flutes and drums. Sarah Elizabeth began to enjoy the banquet again.

When the dance was over, three jugglers appeared. Their performance with flaming torches was exciting to watch. A group of sword dancers followed them, entertaining with great timing and skill. Then, to quiet the room, a harpist began playing a lovely melody, and a poet came forward to recite a long poem in praise of King Auletes.

The king was so pleased with the poet and the entertainers that he gave each of them a gold ring.

It was time now for the birthday presents. The foreign ambassadors took turns presenting their gifts to the king. Their gifts included: jewels, gold and silver, silken materials, exotic birds, lively monkeys, a sleek cheetah, and even a young giraffe.

The king was delighted with all of his gifts, but when Cleopatra gave him the ancient flute, a tear slid down his nose. He squeezed her hand and told her that it was the perfect gift and that he couldn't wait to play it.

The king made Lanata happy by telling her that he would keep his favorite perfumed oil in the little lion bottle. And when Sarah Elizabeth offered him her white flower, the king smiled broadly and said, "This is a surprise! You are the little friend of Saphira. How sweet and forgiving you are to give me such a beautiful flower on my birthday."

After the king had received his gifts, hot mint tea was given to everyone. As Cleopatra reached for her tea, she noticed that Berenice was smiling at her. Looking down, she saw that she was holding a silver goblet instead of her usual golden one. In an instant, she spilled some of the tea on the table. The liquid began to sizzle and smoke, eating its way into the table. Jason and Madrian saw at once what had happened, but when they turned toward Berenice, she was gone.

"We haven't heard the last of this from my dear sister," Cleopatra said. "Do not leave Sarah Elizabeth's side, Jason; you must not sleep tonight. Let us not speak of this to my father as I do not wish to spoil his birthday." Cleopatra poured the remaining poison into an empty container near the table. She motioned to a servant. "Take this container and bury it and its poisonous contents. As for the silver goblet, clean it thoroughly and return it to me. It will serve as a reminder of one who would have me dead."

CHAPTER 11
Alexander the Great's Library

Sarah Elizabeth had awakened several times in the night with bad dreams. Each time, Jason was still sitting by her side. Once in her dreams, she saw an evil-looking man coming toward her with a knife. Jason said something just as the knife was raised to strike her, and she awakened.

She was glad that it was morning now and time to get up. Cleopatra had promised to take her to see the great library in Alexandria today. It would be a lovely day, and she would forget her nightmares.

As Sarah Elizabeth, Lanata and Jason walked into the hall outside their bed chamber, Sarah Elizabeth noticed a statue of stone which made her shiver all over. With its upraised arm and knife, it reminded her of the man in her dream. "I don't remember that statue, Lanata. Has it always been there?"

"I have never seen it before, Sarah Elizabeth. I don't like looking at it. I wonder if Cleopatra knows it is here." Lanata wrinkled her nose in disgust.

"Have you seen it before, Jason?" asked Sarah Elizabeth, looking very carefully at him.

"What's that, Sarabeth? I'm afraid my mind has been on other things."

"I asked if you had seen this statue before."

"It does look slightly familiar, but it's all wrong for this hall, much too grim. Why don't we have Cleopatra send it to her sister?" Jason had a gleam in his eye.

During breakfast, Jason and Cleopatra had a private chat. There was much nodding of heads and a good deal of laughter. Sarah Elizabeth saw Cleopatra call two of her servants and gesture with her arm raised upward. The servants quickly left the room as if on important business.

After breakfast, Cleopatra, Jason and the dolls rode in a beautiful chariot, accompanied by the royal guards to the library. Since Madrian had work to do elsewhere, Cleopatra said she would be their guide. She loved the library very much. It had been Alexander the Great's library. It was very beautiful and absolutely enormous. High and airy with many windows, it would be a wonderful place in which to study.

"Do you see the scrolls of papyrus in the open cabinets, Sarah Elizabeth?" asked Cleopatra. "They record all of man's history and learning from the beginning of time. There are 700,000 of them."

"That's amazing, Cleopatra. Tell me, is it true that papyrus is made from an Egyptian plant?"

"Yes, my dear, you have probably seen pretty papyrus plants growing near the ponds in the palace gardens. Strips of their stems are used to make an excellent writing material. Do you see that man in the gray robe sitting over there? He is my Greek teacher, a very great scholar. I must admit that most of the time I really feel more Greek than Egyptian. I suppose it is because of my ancestors."

"Speaking of Greeks," said Jason, "the library has a fascinating section on Greek architecture. Of course, I must admit to being partial to the section on bears."

"Well, I prefer the information about dolls," said Lanata, who had been dying to get a word in edgewise. "I do wish they had more information about dolls from other parts of the world. Sarah Elizabeth, if you could stay longer in Egypt, we could work together on a new scroll about dolls. Is that possible?" Lanata smiled at Sarah Elizabeth.

"I'd love that, Lanata, but Jason says we must leave soon. It's such a good idea for a project. Maybe Cleopatra could help you with it."

Cleopatra took the dolls by the hands saying, "Of course I will help, but let us not think of departures yet; there is still so much to see. Now we are going to visit the museum and the tomb of Alexander the Great. Then, if there is still time, we'll have a picnic on the hill outside the Temple of Serapis, where we can see a beautiful view of the Nile as it flows into the sea."

By the time the day was over, Sarah Elizabeth had been through the greatest learning center in the Ancient World. She had heard stories about the students and inventors who had come from all over the world to study at the Alexandrian Library. Cleopatra had even taken the time to teach Sarah Elizabeth how to read and write some of the Egyptian picture writing. The doll would have so many things to tell her family when she returned home.

CHAPTER 12
Temper Tantrums

Berenice was in a rage. She had been screaming at her servants ever since the stone statue had arrived at her chamber in the palace.

She didn't know how Cleopatra had turned her man to stone, but she would get even. She would take care of Cleopatra and that nasty visiting doll at the same time. In fact, she would get rid of the whole crowd: Madrian, Iras, Charmian, Lanata and that awful fuzzy-faced bear. She would have them all poisoned, drowned or locked up in cages. How dare they spoil her plans? For Cleopatra – a special death – the Nile River CROCODILES!

"Cleopatra thinks she's so beautiful. Anyone can see that she has the face of a toad. Do you not agree, Craxat?" Berenice was shrieking at her ancient servant.

"Oh yes, Madam, you should take the boat."

"Not boat, you ninny, I said she has the face of a toad!"

"Yes, Yes, Madam, you should go on the road."

"One more word out of you, Craxat, and I'll boil you in oil." Berenice began to hurl her perfume bottles at the servant, who with better wisdom than hearing, scuttled out of the room.

Berenice began shrieking for another servant. "Yaya! Yaya! Where is that man?"

"Here I am, Madam, at your service." A sly-looking man came slithering into the room.

"Yaya," said Berenice, adjusting her wig which had begun to slip during her tantrum. "I want you to get twenty of my most vicious henchmen together. They are to seize Cleopatra, her servants, the dolls and that horrible bear and bring them to me. And don't forget that revolting little Madrian. You can rough them up as much as you wish, but I want them alive. I have many pretty tortures waiting for them." Berenice's eyes glittered with wickedness. "Bring them to me tonight or you will wish you were never born."

"So be it, Most Divine Princess. Yaya, your loyal servant, is honored that you have chosen me to take care of your enemies. I would gladly give my undeserving life for you, most beautiful lady. Count on Yaya. I will always…"

"Get on with it, Yaya, less talk and more action. I see through your flattery."

Yaya hurried from the room, grateful to be away from his mistress, who might dent his head with a vase as a parting gesture. He would do as commanded, and maybe she would give him some gold coins which would be useful in paying his debts. Of course, if he could turn Madrian over to her, he would not be so in debt. He never seemed to learn that the dwarf could always beat him in games of chance. Yes, he would go after Madrian first.

CHAPTER 13
Evil in the Palace

King Auletes had left during the day for Rome. The palace was much quieter since he had taken many of his servants with him. Cleopatra had decided to have dinner served in her chamber. She had invited the dolls and Jason to join her. This would be their last dinner together since Jason was taking Sarah Elizabeth home on the following day. Madrian, Charmian and Iras were with them. Even little Saphira was on hand. Cleopatra had ordered a special meal with honey cakes for Jason and orange ambrosia for Sarah Elizabeth.

It had been a happy evening with very little talk of their departure. After dinner, Sarah Elizabeth asked if she might take a walk in the garden for one last look at the lovely Egyptian night sky. Lanata said she would walk with her. The others were busy talking with each other.

Lanata was just pointing out her favorite stars to Sarah Elizabeth, who was holding Saphira, when the dolls heard muffled footsteps coming toward them.

"Shh, Lanata, let's hide behind these bushes. Don't make a sound."

The dolls held their breath as a large gang of men passed by them.

"Sarah Elizabeth, what should we do? I'm sure they are heading for Cleopatra's chamber. The man in the lead is Berenice's awful henchman, Yaya."

"Come with me, Lanata. We'll follow them, keeping our distance, of course. If there's trouble, we may be of some help." The dolls tiptoed quietly after the villains.

As the gang reached Cleopatra's chamber, they overpowered the guards and burst into the room with daggers drawn. Two of them grabbed Cleopatra and threatened to kill her on the spot if anyone made a move. In a flash, they had tied up everyone.

"Where are the dolls? Our mistress insists that we bring back the dolls, too."

"Dolls? What dolls?" Madrian looked at Jason. "Have you seen any dolls?"

"No dolls today, old chap. There were some in the palace yesterday, but I think they went to Rome with the king. Yes, I remember hearing them talking about going to Rome. What a shame they are missing this party. They love parties." Jason winked at Madrian.

Cleopatra glared at Yaya. "Untie me, you maniac. The king will have you killed for doing this to me."

Yaya tied a filthy rag around Cleopatra's mouth. "He'll never know what happened to you. By the time he returns, you will have vanished without a trace. Your sister intends to feed you to the crocodiles." Yaya grinned wickedly as he said this.

Sarah Elizabeth and Lanata had been listening outside in the garden. They hid under a stone bench as the gang dragged Cleopatra and the others past them. Then they crept after them, making sure that they were far enough away to keep from being seen. Sarah Elizabeth couldn't understand why Jason had not put an end to this mischief, but she knew he must have his reasons.

81

When the gang reached the darkened area of the palace, they shoved their victims into a small room. Then Yaya went to get Berenice, leaving the largest thug in command. Moments later, Berenice entered the room. She could hardly contain her joy at seeing Cleopatra in her power.

"Soooo dear sister, we meet again. How does it feel to have your mouth shut for once? Something tells me you don't like this situation at all. Did Yaya tell you that I have a special swim in the river planned for you and your friends?"

Cleopatra's eyes were flashing fury at Berenice, and she tried desperately to break her bonds.

"It's useless to struggle, sister dear. I must leave you now in order to get a fine reward for my brave helpers, but I will return soon to settle with you." Berenice gave Cleopatra a look that would have frozen the desert sun.

It was all Sarah Elizabeth could do to keep Lanata from attacking Berenice. "Not yet, Lanata. I will give you a signal when it's time. We must let Jason and Madrian know that we are here. I know, Lanata, Saphira can bring them a message."

"How, Sarah Elizabeth? We have no writing materials."

"I have a bracelet Jason gave me. Saphira can bring it to him. Jason will know that we are near." As she said this, Sarah Elizabeth put her scarab bracelet around the kitten's neck, gave her a little pat and told her to go to Jason. The kitten moved quietly toward the open door.

Because of her tiny size, it was easy for Saphira to get past the men at the door. She kept in the shadow until she found Jason, who was tied up in a corner of the room. She rubbed her neck against his paws until he could feel the bracelet. Jason understood and smiled at the kitten. Then he twitched his nose, and his bonds slid to the floor. He moved swiftly from one captive to another, loosening their bonds with just a slight touch of his paw. He whispered to them to pretend they were still tied up until he gave them a signal.

Just then Yaya entered the room and stood over Madrian gloating. "I'll teach you to beat me in a game. Your games are over Madrian. I'll be paying my gambling debt to you in a way you never expected." Yaya gave Madrian a vicious kick.

This was too much for Madrian, who grabbed Yaya's ankle and gave it a ferocious bite. Yaya screamed and the men outside jammed the doorway as they tried to get inside to see what was happening. Madrian had Yaya on the ground and was wrestling him for his dagger.

As the men began to push their way into the room, Jason stood up. There was a blinding flash, and at that instant, the men had been turned into tiny game pieces.

In a firm yet gentle voice, Jason said, "Madrian, don't damage Yaya too much, we'll need a game board. Iras and Charmian, there is no need to be frightened. The danger is over for now. Pick up the game pieces and put them on the table."

Cleopatra was beginning to compose herself. At the same time, she was looking at Jason with amazement.

"The best is yet to come, Your Highness. Be patient just a little longer." Jason brought Saphira over to her.

Sarah Elizabeth and Lanata had heard Yaya screaming, but Sarah Elizabeth had a plan which she'd whispered to Lanata. They were staying hidden in the garden.

Presently, Berenice returned carrying a heavy bag of coins. As she drew near, Sarah Elizabeth shouted, "NOW!" and the dolls jumped from the shadows.

Berenice let out a yelp as she felt something yanking her robe. She reached down to push it away, and Lanata, attacking from behind, gave her wig a shove over her eyes. Since Berenice could no longer see, she fell to the ground and began to plead for mercy.

"Get up, get up, you wicked woman. Stop your sniveling." Lanata tugged at her until she got to her feet.

"What do you suppose is taking Berenice so long?" asked Jason. As he looked toward the door, he saw the two small dolls leading a quivering Berenice into the room.

Cleopatra bristled as she saw her sister. "By the Sacred Baboon, you've really done it now, Berenice. We'll have to lock you up until Father returns and decides what to do with you."

"Oh dear sister, take pity on me. I have been blinded. I was attacked by wild animals, and I can no longer see." Berenice began to wail.

"Stop your wailing, you silly fool. You haven't lost your eyesight. Your wig is over your eyes. Sometimes I cannot believe your stupidity, Berenice." Cleopatra turned to Madrian who was busily setting up his new game board.

"Madrian, before you get into that game of 'Henchmen,' I want you and Jason to take Berenice to the east wing of the palace. See that she is well guarded. She is to be given food and drink, but she is not to be released until King Auletes has heard of her latest incident."

"Cleopatra," said Lanata, "there is a large bag of gold coins hidden in the berry bush outside. Perhaps Madrian and Jason could pick it up on their way."

"Thank you, Lanata. Attend to the bag, my friends. You may divide it in any way you see fit."

Before leaving the room with Madrian and Berenice, Jason returned the scarab bracelet to Sarah Elizabeth. "Get plenty of sleep tonight, Sarabeth. We have a long journey tomorrow."

CHAPTER 14
The Departure

Sarah Elizabeth was wearing her yellow dress and white bow again, and Jason had removed his headdress. Cleopatra had asked Charmian to pack their Egyptian garments in a travel bag. Only she and Charmian knew that there were some of her rare emeralds hidden within the clothes as her farewell gift to Jason and Sarah Elizabeth.

Cleopatra was still trying to talk them out of leaving. "Wouldn't you like to be permanent members of the Court? Sarah Elizabeth, you can be an honorary princess, and Jason can become my royal advisor."

"Dear Princess, we must decline your generous offer. Sarabeth has obligations to her family, and I must get on with my work in the universe," said Jason.

"Cleopatra, would you be sure to say 'goodbye' to Lanata for me? Tell her that I'll be thinking of her often when I am home." Sarah Elizabeth looked sad as she said this.

"I can't imagine where Lanata can be. She knew that you would be leaving early." Cleopatra looked puzzled. "Please wait a little longer. I am certain that she will be here at any moment." She had just said this when Lanata, breathless and nearly in tears, burst into the room.

"Oh my friends, I am so glad you didn't leave. I couldn't let you go without a gift or two. This one is for you, Jason," said Lanata as she handed him a warm package.

Jason sniffed the air as he unwrapped his gift. "Honey cakes for the trip! How marvelous! How thoughtful! How delicious!" Jason gave Lanata a great big "bear-hug."

"And this is for you, Sarah Elizabeth," said Lanata, handing her a small leather pouch which was tied with a golden cord.

Sarah Elizabeth untied the cord and reached into the pouch, pulling out a strange wooden object with tiny beads. "Lanata! It's an ancient doll – a wooden paddle doll! I saw one in a museum once. Are you really giving it to me?"

"Yes, Sarah Elizabeth, it is yours. The king gave a special privilege, saying that he knew the doll would be well taken care of and appreciated by you."

Sarah Elizabeth gave Lanata a hug equal to the one she had received from Jason. "I will treasure it forever, Lanata. Please thank King Auletes for me, too."

The gifts were carefully placed within the travel bag. Then after another round of hugs, which included Cleopatra, Madrian, Iras and Charmian, and, of course, Saphira, Jason said, "We really must leave now, but we will never forget you."

He hoisted the bag to his shoulder, and taking Sarah Elizabeth by the hand, moved into the garden.

As they walked down the path, the Egyptian friends could hear Jason's growly voice chanting:

"Wings of gold and crystal bells,
Starlight in the night,
Take us swiftly through the years,
As we fade from sight."

CHAPTER 15
Home Again

Sarah Elizabeth looked about the garden. Gone were the papyrus plants, the palm trees and exotic birds. In their place were the forget-me-nots, tiny pink roses and the hummingbirds of her very own garden. She wondered where Jason could be.

On the wooden bench by the big pine tree, she saw the remains of a honey cake, her Egyptian dress folded neatly and a small leather pouch tied with a golden cord. Sarah Elizabeth picked up the pouch and untied the cord. Reaching inside, she found the small wooden paddle doll and two very beautiful green emeralds.

A gift from Cleopatra?

(And who was that looking down at her from a high branch in the tree?)

All the memories of her exciting stay in ancient Egypt came flooding back to her. She couldn't wait to write them in her diary. She wondered if Kristi would be home or away at the university. She was eager to tell her this latest adventure and to show her the strange little doll, the emeralds and her dress.

Sarah Elizabeth wondered how long she had been gone. It was confusing because it seemed as if it had been both a short and a long time. She felt happy but tired. She carefully put the emeralds and the little doll back in the leather pouch. Carrying the pouch and the Egyptian dress, she walked across the garden to her house. As she started up the stairs, two furry shapes rushed down to greet her. Tuptim and Blackberry, her two pretty cats, meowed and purred and rubbed against her.

Sarah Elizabeth remembered Aunt Fluffy. She would have to tell her cats all about the Sacred White Cat, but maybe she could take a little nap first.

When she entered the house, the cats followed her. No one was home yet, so she went into the bedroom. First, she put the leather pouch and her scarab bracelet in a drawer in her bureau. Then she hung the Egyptian dress in the closet. Finally, she lay down on her little bed. The cats curled up on the rug near her bed. Sarah Elizabeth fell fast asleep as the cats purred softly with pleasure that she was home once more.

CPSIA information can be obtained at www.ICGtesting.com
Printed in the USA
BVOW01s0444090315

390578BV00006B/10/P